How Rotten!

The girls and Hannah parted ways just inside the festival. Hannah wandered off to look at some craft booths, while Nancy, George, and Bess headed for the information board.

As they started discussing what to do first, the three girls heard a shout from nearby. Nancy looked up and saw Mr. Helmer rushing up to a pair of T-shirted festival workers. The orchard owner looked very upset.

"Uh-oh," Nancy whispered to her friends. "I wonder what's wrong?"

It wasn't long before she had the answer to her question. Mr. Helmer stopped in front of the workers.

"This is terrible!" he cried, waving his hands in the air. "Someone stole my River Heights Reds!"

The Nancy Drew Notebooks

Available from Simon & Schuster

THE
NANCY DREW
NOTEBOOKS®

#68

The Apple Bandit

CAROLYN KEENE
ILLUSTRATED BY JAN NAIMO JONES

Aladdin Paperbacks
New York   London   Toronto   Sydney

This book is a work of fiction. Any references to historical events, real
people, or real locales are used fictitiously. Other names, characters,
places, and incidents are the product of the author's imagination, and
any resemblance to actual events or locales or persons, living or dead,
is entirely coincidental.

❦ ALADDIN PAPERBACKS
An imprint of Simon & Schuster Children's Publishing Division
1230 Avenue of the Americas, New York, NY 10020
Copyright © 2005 by Simon & Schuster, Inc
ALADDIN PAPERBACKS, NANCY DREW, THE NANCY DREW
NOTEBOOKS, and colophon are trademarks of Simon and Schuster, Inc.
Designed by Lisa Vega
The text of this book was set in Excelsior.
Manufactured in the United States of America
First Aladdin Paperbacks Edition October 2005
    4 6 8 10 9 7 5 3
Library of Congress Control Number 2005922886
ISBN-13: 978-1-4169-0829-6
ISBN-10: 1-4169-0829-3

1

Apple Fun

"Apples, apples, apples! I love apples!" Bess Marvin chanted.

"Would you stop saying that?" George Fayne grumbled. "By the time we get there, I'm not going to want to hear anything else about apples, ever!"

Eight-year-old Nancy Drew grinned at her two best friends, who were also cousins. The three of them were sitting in the backseat of Mrs. Fayne's car as it drove down a country road.

"Uh-oh, George," Nancy teased. "That's bad news, since we're going to the River Heights Kids *Apple* Festival!"

George's mom smiled at the three girls in the rearview mirror. "That's right," she said. "And we're almost there. Nancy, you'd better make sure Chip is on her leash before we get out of the car, okay?"

"Okay." Nancy leaned down and patted her puppy, Chocolate Chip. She was lying on the car floor on top of Nancy's feet.

"Did you hear that, Chip?" Bess said. "You have to stay on your leash. There will probably be lots of other dogs at the Apple Festival. Some of them might not be as friendly as you are."

When she heard Bess say her name, Chip let out a bark. She jumped onto Nancy's lap, then bounced over to George's.

"Quit it." George giggled, pushing the wriggling puppy onto Bess. "Chip, your claws tickle!"

Nancy reached over and clipped Chip's leash to her collar. "There," she said. "Now we're ready to go."

"Good," Mrs. Fayne said. "Because we're here!"

It was a bright, sunny Friday afternoon in autumn. Mrs. Fayne stopped the car in the parking lot of a pick-your-own fruit farm. In the summer people came from miles around to pick their own fresh berries, peaches, cherries, and other produce. In the autumn they came for the juicy apples and pears.

"Now, don't go crazy, Bess," Mrs. Fayne joked. "Make sure you leave enough apples for everybody else in town."

"Fat chance!" George said with a laugh. "When Bess is around, nobody else in the family ever gets to eat an apple."

"Or apple pie," Mrs. Fayne added.

"Or applesauce," Nancy joined in with a grin.

Bess giggled. "Or apple cider, or apple turnovers, or apple brown betty . . ."

Still laughing, they walked over to the ticket booth.

"I'll buy you girls each a weekend pass," Mrs. Fayne said as she handed some money to the ticket taker. "You still want to come back tomorrow, right?"

"Definitely!" Bess answered.

Nancy nodded. They knew they would only have a short time today before it got dark, but tomorrow they could have the whole day here.

"We definitely need to come back tomorrow," she said. "Otherwise we'll never have enough time to see everything."

"Or taste everything," Bess added.

"Okay, then." Mrs. Fayne handed each girl a ticket. "Hold on to these. Ready to go inside?"

"Ready!" the girls all cried.

Nancy kept a tight hold on Chip's leash as she entered the festival grounds. There were lots of dogs everywhere inside—and lots of people, too.

The festival entrance was in a big, open area in front of an old farmhouse. To one side were rows and rows of fruit trees. Sprinklers were spraying water along several of the rows. Nancy guessed that the orchard workers had to water the trees when the weather was dry and sunny, as it had been for the past couple of weeks.

On the other side of the central area there was a grassy hillside. It led up toward steep, wooded bluffs at the back of the property. Nearby stood a large red barn and several other outbuildings. For the festival several tents and food stands were set up here and there.

"Look, there's an information board." George pointed to a large bulletin board covered with a map and lots of other signs and notices. The heading INFORMATION was written across the top in big red letters.

Nancy followed her friends over to the information board. She had to keep trying to pull Chip away from other dogs walking by.

"Quit it, Chip." Nancy pointed to a big, handwritten notice on the sign. "All dogs have to stay on leash. See? It says so right there."

Chip barked. Then she sat down on Nancy's feet and wagged her tail.

"My dad told me that the owner of this farm has a bunch of big dogs that run around loose all the time," Bess said. "He said the farm dogs are nice to people, but they chase away other animals. They're supposed to guard the fruit from raccoons and groundhogs and stuff."

"I guess that's probably one reason other dogs aren't allowed to be off their leashes," Nancy said, looking down at Chip.

Just then Mrs. Fayne smiled and waved to someone in the crowd. "There's Mrs. Karoli over there," she told the girls. "I'm going to go over and say hello. Will you three be all right on your own for a while?"

"Sure, Mom," George replied. "We'll be fine."

"Okay. Stay together at all times," Mrs. Fayne told them. "We'll meet right back here at four forty-five. And please keep a tight hold on Chip, okay?"

"Don't worry, we will," Nancy promised. "See you at four forty-five."

After Mrs. Fayne left, the girls looked at the information board again. Now that she was closer, Nancy saw a printed schedule of events, several notices advertising different games and food booths, and even a poster about pony rides.

"I don't know what we should do first," George said. "Should we get a snack, or play some games first?"

"Snack first," Bess suggested, licking her lips eagerly.

"I wouldn't mind checking out the pony rides," Nancy added. She and her friends loved ponies and sometimes took riding lessons at a local stable.

"Ooh! Look! It says there are hayrides,

too," Bess said. "Oh, now I really can't decide what we should do!"

"Sounds like we have a real mystery on our hands," Nancy joked. "Maybe I should get out my notebook."

She patted her pocket. That was where she had tucked her mystery notebook.

Nancy loved to solve mysteries. She was good at it too. She always wrote down the clues and suspects for each new case in her special notebook. Nancy wasn't really expecting to find a mystery at the Apple Festival. But she knew that mysteries could pop up where she least expected, so she liked to carry her notebook with her all the time—just in case.

"Ha-ha, very funny," Bess said with a smile. "I think we can figure this one out without your notebook. Maybe we should stop at the food stand for a quick snack of cider and donuts, and then—"

"No!" George interrupted loudly. She stabbed one finger at the board, looking anxious. "We have to hurry!"

2

The Applesauce-Eating Contest

What?" Nancy nervously asked George. "What's wrong?"

"Look!" George pointed again.

Nancy read the sign her friend pointed to:

APPLESAUCE–EATING CONTEST

COME ONE, COME ALL!

EVERY DAY ON THE FARMHOUSE PORCH.

SHOW OFF YOUR EATING ABILITY AND

WIN PRIZES.

WINNERS FROM EACH DAY'S CONTEST

WILL COMPETE AGAINST ONE ANOTHER IN

THE BIG FINALE.

The sign continued:

GRAND PRIZE:
A BUSHEL OF THE VERY NEW, VERY RARE,
VERY DELICIOUS RIVER HEIGHTS RED:
A BRAND-NEW VARIETY OF APPLE GROWN
RIGHT HERE AT OUR ORCHARD!
BE THE FIRST ONE IN TOWN TO TASTE THIS
OUTSTANDING NEW APPLE!

At the bottom of the notice was a list of times for different age groups on different days. Nancy gasped. "Bess, you should enter this! You'd win for sure."

"No duh," George said. "But look, her age group is starting in less than five minutes!"

Bess was already rushing off into the crowd. "Come on!" she cried over her shoulder. "We have to hurry!"

The three girls raced toward the farmhouse. Chip loped along at Nancy's heels, panting happily.

They arrived just in time to sign up Bess for the contest. "Whew!" George said as a festival worker handed Bess a contestant's badge. "That was close!"

The festival worker smiled. "You'd better get up there and find a seat," she told Bess. "The contest will be starting any minute now. Good luck!"

"She won't need luck," George told the worker confidently. "Bess is an apple-eating machine!"

Bess giggled. She thanked the festival worker and hurried up the porch steps. There was a long table set up on the porch, and Nancy counted ten other kids already seated behind it.

Nancy and George found a spot to sit on the grass in front of the porch. There were lots of other people watching too.

"Good luck, Bess!" Nancy shouted to her friend, shifting Chip's leash to her other hand.

Bess waved and smiled as she sat down. "Thanks, Nancy!" she called back.

Meanwhile George was checking out Bess's competition. "Look, there's Phoebe Archer," she whispered, nudging Nancy. "And Kyle Leddington, too."

Nancy nodded. "Isn't that Laura Anderson from the other third-grade class sitting at the end?" she asked.

"Probably," George replied. "The sign said second and third graders are in this group."

"I don't recognize most of the other kids," Nancy said. "They must go to other schools."

"Yeah," George agreed. "Luckily, most of them don't look like big eaters. Especially that kid." She pointed to a short, skinny boy with red hair who was seated on Bess's left.

Nancy felt her arm jerk to the side as Chip jumped up and barked. When she turned to see what the puppy was barking at, Nancy saw George's mother walking toward them.

"Hi, girls," Mrs. Fayne said. "Having fun so far?"

"Look, Mom," George said, pointing to the porch. "Bess just entered the applesauce-eating contest!"

"Oh, my." Mrs. Fayne laughed. "I hope those other kids know what they're up against!"

Just then a tall, ruddy-faced man wearing overalls stepped up onto the porch. He was smiling and holding a microphone.

"Hello, everyone!" he said. "I'm John

13

Helmer, the owner of this orchard. Welcome to the second-and-third-grade heat of our applesauce-eating contest!"

The crowd cheered. The contestants on the porch clapped and smiled.

"Go, Bess!" George shouted.

"Whooo!" Nancy cheered as loudly as she could.

Even Chip joined in by barking.

Finally Mr. Helmer held up his hands, and the crowd quieted down again. "Okay, before we get started, I thought our contestants should know what they're playing for," he said with a wink. "May I present the River Heights Red!"

He reached into the pocket of his overalls and pulled out a large, shiny red apple. Setting it on the end of the long table, he opened a pocketknife and quickly sliced it into a dozen pieces.

"The winner of each heat will get the chance to compete for a whole bushel of these beauties," he said. "Now, I'm going to give the contestants a little taste."

He handed out the apple slices to the

kids on the porch. Nancy watched as Bess popped her slice into her mouth.

"Wow!" Bess shouted loudly as soon as she'd chewed and swallowed. "That apple tastes great!"

The watching crowd laughed. "Bess sure does love apples," Mrs. Fayne commented.

Mr. Helmer smiled at Bess. "I'm glad you like it," he said.

"Like it? I love it!" Bess declared. "Now I *know* I'm going to win this contest—I'd do anything for a whole bushel of those apples!"

"No way!" Kyle Leddington called out. "*I'm* going to win those apples!"

"No, me!" several others added.

Mr. Helmer chuckled as the crowd laughed again. "Sounds like it's a good thing I have that prize bushel of River Heights Reds hidden away out of sight!" he teased. "Especially with this young lady around!" He pointed at Bess.

Nancy smiled, but she was distracted by a loud bark nearby. She glanced over, just in case a dog was coming toward Chip.

She saw a large dalmatian, sitting quietly at its owner's feet. Then she saw another woman standing near the dalmatian.

The woman looked a little older than Nancy's dad. She was wearing a brown jacket with pictures of fruit all over it and leaning on a carved wooden walking stick. She was staring up at the porch, just like the rest of the crowd. But instead of smiling or cheering like everyone else, she was scowling angrily.

That's strange, Nancy thought. *She doesn't look like she's having much fun. . . .*

Just then Mr. Helmer announced that the contest was about to start. Returning her attention to the porch, Nancy saw several festival workers holding huge trays stacked with big bowls of applesauce. They set a bowl in front of each contestant.

"Ready . . . set . . . go!" Mr. Helmer cried.

Up on the porch the contestants eagerly began slurping the applesauce. Bess kept her face close to the bowl, scooping up spoonful after spoonful without pausing for breath.

16

"Go, Bess!" Nancy screamed at the top of her lungs.

All around her the rest of the crowd was yelling too. Excited by the noise, Chip ran around Nancy until her leash was all tangled. But Nancy hardly noticed. She kept her gaze trained on Bess, even as she stepped out of the leash loop.

"She's winning! She's winning!" George shrieked.

"Go, Bess! Eat, girl!" Mrs. Fayne yelled.

"And we have a winner!" Mr. Helmer stepped forward, clapping his hands and moving along behind the contestants.

Nancy gasped. "What?" she cried. "Did Bess finish?"

But instead of stopping behind Bess, Mr. Helmer stepped over to the skinny, red-haired boy. He patted him on the head.

"Excellent eating, young man," Mr. Helmer said. "You have the best time so far today!"

The boy lifted both skinny arms over his head. His face was covered in goopy applesauce.

The crowd cheered. Nancy clapped politely, even though she was disappointed that Bess hadn't won.

"Oh, well," she said. "It looks like Bess probably came in second, at least."

"Yes, she did very well," Mrs. Fayne agreed.

George scowled. "Rats," she said. "I wanted her to win. Now she won't get a prize—she ate all that applesauce for nothing!"

Her mother chuckled. "Oh, I wouldn't say that," she said. "For Bess, the applesauce was probably its own reward."

Up on the porch Mr. Helmer told the winner to come back the next day for the finals. Then he pulled a sheaf of papers out of his pocket.

"As for the rest of you, very good job," he said. "As a consolation prize, I have festival coupons for all of you. You can use them for the hayride, or the pony rides, or the other games and activities this weekend. Thanks for playing!"

3

Pony Paradise

Well, that was fun," Mrs. Fayne said. "I'll see you girls again at four forty-five as we planned, all right?"

"Right," George said.

"Nancy, do you want me to take Chip for a while?" Mrs. Fayne added. "If you girls want to use Bess's coupon on the pony rides, it's probably better if Chip doesn't come along."

Nancy glanced down at her puppy. Chip's leash was tangled around her ankles again. "Oh, that's true," she said. "That would be great—if you don't mind taking her."

"Not at all." Mrs. Fayne smiled and

helped Nancy untangle herself. Then she took Chip's leash, waved, and headed off into the crowd.

Nancy and George walked toward the porch to meet Bess. It felt a little strange not to have to watch out for Chip. But Nancy soon forgot about that when she saw Bess's disappointed, applesauce-covered face.

"You did great," Nancy told her. "Um, I would give you a hug. But . . . you know." She giggled and pointed to the applesauce dripping from Bess's chin and down her front.

Bess looked down and smiled. "Oops," she said. "Oh well. I can't believe I didn't win!"

"Me neither," George agreed. "But at least you got that coupon. Where do you want to use it?"

"Pony rides," Bess said immediately. "Seeing some cute ponies will help me forget that I won't be getting those River Heights Reds." She licked her lips. "That's one delicious apple! I wish I knew where Mr. Helmer was hiding them so I could sneak one!"

Nancy grinned. She knew her friend was joking—Bess would never actually steal anything, even an apple. But it was obvious that she'd really enjoyed her bite of the River Heights Red.

"Maybe you can talk your parents into buying you some," she said. "I think they're going on sale right after the festival."

One of the festival workers handed a paper towel to Bess. She wiped her face. Then the girls went back to the information board to find out where the pony rides were.

"There they are on the map." George pointed. "It looks like they're way up at the top of the hill."

Nancy turned and looked up the steep hill that rose along one side of the farmhouse. "They probably put the rides way up there so the noise of the festival doesn't bother the ponies," she guessed.

George giggled. "And so the smell of the ponies doesn't bother the festival," she added. "Come on, let's go check it out!"

The girls started climbing the hill. Along the way they passed several food stands.

Nancy and George stopped to buy apple turnovers. But Bess shook her head when they offered her some.

"No, thanks," she said. "I'm so full from all that applesauce that I—"

She was interrupted by a flurry of loud barks, followed by an angry shout. "Uh-oh," George said. "What's going on up there?"

Nancy didn't answer. She was looking ahead at several large, barking dogs. An angry-looking young woman wearing a River Heights Kids Apple Festival T-shirt was shouting at a pair of teenage boys who stood in front of her. Apples littered the ground nearby.

"I wonder what's happening," Bess whispered, sounding a little nervous.

Nancy's detective mind was already putting two and two together. "Those must be the farm dogs," she whispered back. "I bet those kids were messing around with them or something, and got caught."

Just then Mr. Helmer came rushing up the hill. "What is it, Sandy?" he asked the woman in the T-shirt.

She pointed to the boys. "These hooligans were picking apples off the trees in the orchard without paying for them," she said. "Then they were using them to play fetch with your dogs."

"Nancy, you were right," George whispered.

Nancy smiled. Even if it was a small mystery, it was still fun to solve it. She listened as Mr. Helmer scolded the boys.

". . . and I'm afraid you're not welcome at the festival anymore," he finished sternly. "You'll have to leave now."

"Whatever," one of the boys muttered. "It's boring here anyway."

"Yeah, but you better watch it," the other boy spoke up sullenly. "It's not very nice to kick out your customers. I'm going to tell my parents never to buy your apples again!"

"Especially your stupid River Heights Red," the first boy added. "I bet it tastes like dirt!"

"All right, that's enough." Mr. Helmer's voice sounded angry. "Let's go, boys."

As he marched them off down the hill,

Nancy and her friends looked at one another. "Wow," Bess said. "Those boys were troublemakers!"

"Never mind them," George said. "Let's go see the ponies. It's getting late!"

The girls continued on their way. At the top of the hill, they saw a round pen set up in a small but pretty meadow. Four cute, shaggy ponies were walking around the outside, led by several teenage girls. A few trees provided shade at one end of the pen, and nearby someone had set up a large water tub and a pile of hay. Several people were standing in line waiting for rides, while others were looking at the hilly scenery on the far side of the pen.

"Wow, there's a good view from up here," Nancy said. She walked past the pony pen to get a better look over the side of the hill. She saw a large, fast-moving creek below.

George followed, though she stayed well back from the edge. "Yeah," she said. "Just don't fall over that cliff. It's a long way down!"

Bess was more interested in the ponies than the view. "Aren't they adorable?" she cooed. "And look at their nice little pen! This is a great place for ponies."

Nancy giggled. "Yeah," she agreed. "Grass, water, sun—it's practically a pony paradise!"

One of the pony-ride workers overheard Nancy. Her nametag read MARCIE.

"It is nice here, isn't it?" she said with a smile. "I bet our ponies are happy they get to spend the whole weekend here instead of their boring old pasture."

"You mean they're staying here overnight, too?" Bess asked.

The older girl nodded. "That way we don't have to bring them back and forth for each day of the festival."

Marcie hurried off to help the next customer onto a pony. Nancy and her friends took their places at the end of the line.

Nancy noticed that Bess was staring at the coupon in her hand, frowning a little. "Are you still upset about the contest?" Nancy asked.

Bess shrugged. "Not really," she said. "That red-haired kid could really eat." She smiled. "And it was fun, even if I didn't win."

"Good." Suddenly Nancy remembered the scowling woman in the fruit jacket. "Hey, but I noticed one person who wasn't having much fun." She quickly described the woman to her friends.

George nodded. "I saw her too," she said. "That's Mrs. Cherry. She owns that other orchard over near the river. You know— Fruity Acres? My parents know her."

"Really?" Nancy said. "Does she always look that grumpy?"

George shrugged. "I don't think so," she said. "Maybe she's upset that there are so many people here at the festival. She might be worried about losing all her customers."

By now the girls were getting closer to the front of the line. Bess was paying more attention to the passing ponies than to her friends' conversation.

"Ooh, I like that one." Bess pointed to a shaggy little brown-and-white pinto pony. "He's so sweet!"

Marcie happened to be leading a different pony past them just then. She heard what Bess had said and smiled. "Are you talking about H-Two-Oh?" she asked. "He's everyone's favorite."

Bess wrinkled her nose. "H-Two-Oh?" she repeated as the girl moved on out of earshot. "That's a funny name for a pony."

"That *is* a funny name," Nancy said. "H-Two-Oh—that's another way to say 'water.' Who names a pony Water? Do you think we heard her wrong?"

"I don't know." George grinned. "Does this count as a mystery?"

But Bess wasn't listening. She had turned away from the ponies and was staring over the edge of the drop-off.

"Hey!" she cried, suddenly sounding excited. "Look, you guys! I just solved the mystery!"

4

Another Mystery

"**H**uh?" Nancy asked, confused. "What mystery? Do you mean the mystery of the pony's funny name? I thought we were joking about that."

"No, no." Bess waved her hands impatiently. "Come and look at this!"

Nancy and George stepped over to look down the hill to where Bess was pointing. "What?" George asked. "What are we supposed to be looking at? Trees? The creek? What?"

"No, lean this way a little." Bess moved aside to give her friends room. "Now look straight down, about halfway toward the creek."

Nancy gasped as she finally saw what Bess was talking about. "Hey, are those apples down there?"

Sure enough, there were several wooden bushel baskets full of bright red apples tucked into a little plateau on the steep hillside. The apples were almost completely hidden from view by the trees and bushes. But by looking down from their special spot, it was easy for Nancy, Bess, and George to see them.

"Those must be the River Heights Reds," Nancy guessed. "Mr. Helmer said he hid them, right?"

Bess nodded. "Right," she said. "That's a pretty good hiding place!"

Nancy glanced over her shoulder at the fat ponies marching around the ring. "I don't know," she joked. "It seems pretty dangerous to me, hiding them so close to the ponies—I bet they love apples!"

"*I* think it's more dangerous to hide them anywhere Bess might find them," George added with a grin.

Bess stuck out her tongue at her cousin. "Very funny," she said. "Come on, we'd better turn around so nobody figures out what we're looking at. I don't want to give away Mr. Helmer's hiding place."

As they turned back to face the ponies, Nancy saw that they were next in line. "I think we're just in time," she said, glancing up at the sky. It was streaked with orange and pink and red as the sun started to set. "It will be getting dark pretty soon."

George checked her watch. "We need to be back down at the entrance to meet Mom in about twenty minutes."

"That gives us plenty of time for our ride," Bess said. "Me first!"

Soon the three girls were aboard three of the ponies. Bess got to ride H_2O, the little pinto with the funny name. Nancy rode on a cute bay pony named Fred, and George got to try a chestnut with white socks, known as Ginger. Since they were the last ones in line, the workers gave them an extra-long ride.

"Thanks," Nancy said as she hopped down from the saddle. "That was fun. And thank you too, Fred." She gave her pony a pat on the neck.

Then she joined her friends. The pony handler, Marcie, had already removed the saddle from one of the ponies and was setting it on the metal rails of the pen.

"Do you have a lot of work to do to get them ready to spend the night here?" George asked her.

"Not too much," Marcie replied. "We just have to untack them and make sure their water tub is full and they have enough hay. Oh, and make sure the gate is shut tight, of course. We don't want loose ponies running down to the orchard to eat all the apples off the trees!"

The three friends giggled. Since Marcie was so friendly, Nancy decided to ask about H_2O's unusual name. Before she could, though, she saw the little spotted pony grab a mouthful of hay from the pile—and dunk it into the water tub! He lifted it up, dripping wet, and slurped it into his mouth. Then he reached for another chunk of hay and did the same thing.

"Look!" Nancy pointed out the pony's

behavior to her friends. "I think I just solved the mystery of H-Two-Oh's funny name."

Marcie heard her and rolled her eyes. "Yeah, that's why they named him H-Two-Oh," she said. "It's cute, but it's kind of a pain in the neck too. H-Two-Oh gets the water in the tub all gunky—we have to dump and refill it every day even if they don't drink it all. Otherwise it looks like a swamp!"

Nancy smiled. Even from where she was standing, she could see that the water in the tub was looking a little murky.

She watched H_2O dunk another bite of hay. Then she heard Bess gasp. "What's wrong?" Nancy asked her friend.

"Is my watch right?" Bess asked, holding it out for her friends to see. "Because if it is, we're late!"

Nancy leaned over to get a closer look at Bess's wrist—her watch said four forty-five on the dot. And it was a five-minute walk back down the hill to their meeting spot.

"Uh-oh," Nancy said. "Come on, we'd better run!"

The three girls said good-bye to Marcie and took off at top speed, racing around the pony pen and down the hill. Most of the other visitors had already left the festival, so there were only a few people left wandering around.

When they reached the entrance, the girls skidded to a stop and looked around. "Hey," George said. "Where's Mom?"

Bess frowned. "Okay, *this* is a real mystery," she said. "She's never late!"

Nancy glanced around the entrance area. There were about a dozen people nearby, but there was no sign of George's mother.

"I wonder where she—," she began.

"Girls! Here I am!" a breathless voice cried.

Nancy turned and saw Mrs. Fayne rushing toward them. Chip was romping along at her heels.

"Mom!" George exclaimed. "Where were you?"

When they got closer, Nancy could see that Chip's brown fur was slicked down and damp-looking. Mrs. Fayne stopped and gave her a guilty smile.

"Sorry I'm late, girls," she said. "Nancy, I'm afraid Chip got away from me—she pulled the leash right out of my hand! I spent the last half hour trying to find her."

Nancy bent down and patted her puppy's soggy head. There was no mystery about where Chip must have been.

"Let me guess," she said with a grin. "You found her in the creek?" Nancy knew that Chip loved to play in the water.

"That's right. She was splashing around and having a great time." Mrs. Fayne sighed. "I'm sorry, Nancy. All this time I was worried that you might lose hold of her. And then *I'm* the one to lose her!"

Nancy smiled. "Don't worry about it," she said. She took hold of Chip's leash, which was soaking wet. "Like my dad says, all's well that ends well."

They walked to Mrs. Fayne's car in the parking lot. While Mrs. Fayne was getting out her keys, Nancy bent down to try to brush some of the water off Chip's coat. She was glad Mrs. Fayne had a blanket Chip could sit on so the whole car wouldn't get wet.

"Naughty puppy," she said. "You know you're not supposed to—hey, what were you eating, Chip?"

George heard her and bent down to see. "What?"

"Oh, nothing." Nancy brushed at Chip's muzzle. "It looks like Chip has a little apple goop around her mouth. I hope she didn't steal someone's applesauce or something— you know how she loves to eat!"

Bess giggled. "That's for sure! Remember the time she ate my mom's straw hat?"

Nancy smiled at the memory. But she couldn't help feeling a little guilty, too. What if Chip really had eaten someone's food? Or stolen an apple off one of the trees, like those mean boys?

"You know, I think I might leave Chip home tomorrow when we come back here," she said as she opened the back door of the car and helped the puppy jump in. "Just in case!"

The next morning the three friends—minus one mischievous puppy—arrived at the Apple Festival bright and early. It was another beautiful autumn day, and the parking lot was already crowded when they pulled in. Today Nancy's housekeeper, Hannah Gruen, had driven them. Hannah had lived with the Drews ever since Nancy was three years old.

"All right, girls," Hannah said as they walked toward the entrance. "Your parents said it was okay for you to walk around by yourselves again. But you have to promise to stick together."

"Don't worry, Hannah, we will," Nancy said.

The girls and Hannah parted ways just inside the festival. Hannah wandered off to look at some craft booths, while Nancy, George, and Bess headed for the information board.

As they started discussing what to do first, the three girls heard a shout from nearby. Nancy looked up and saw Mr. Helmer rushing up to a pair of T-shirted festival workers. The orchard owner looked very upset.

"Uh-oh," Nancy whispered to her friends. "I wonder what's wrong?"

It wasn't long before she had the answer to her question. Mr. Helmer stopped in front of the workers.

"This is terrible!" he cried, waving his hands in the air. "Someone stole my River Heights Reds!"

5

The Missing Apples

Nancy gasped. "Oh, no!" she cried. "You mean those apples we saw in the ravine are gone?"

Mr. Helmer heard her and hurried over. "What did you say, young lady?" he asked. "Did you figure out my hiding place?"

Nancy nodded and gestured to her friends. "We saw them," she said. "Last night, from the pony paddock."

"We guessed they were the secret River Heights Reds," Bess added. "But we weren't sure."

"Well, you guessed right." Mr. Helmer still sounded upset. "I just went to get them—I

was going to display them today before the big eating contest finale. But when I got to the hiding spot, they were gone!"

"Did you leave them out there in the woods all night?" George asked. "Maybe wild animals ate them or something."

"Impossible." Mr. Helmer shook his head. "My dogs patrol the grounds all night. They chase away any varmint that sets paw on the place."

Nancy nodded thoughtfully, remembering the large dogs she'd seen yesterday. Those dogs did look capable of scaring off wild animals.

"Besides," Mr. Helmer went on, "what raccoon or skunk is going to eat those wooden baskets? They're gone too! Nope, I'm afraid the thief is all too human. . . ."

Nancy noticed Mr. Helmer glaring at something behind her. She turned and recognized Mrs. Cherry standing near the entrance. Today Mrs. Cherry wasn't wearing her fruit-print jacket. Instead she wore a sweatshirt with the name of her orchard printed on it.

"Irene!" Mr. Helmer said, striding toward her. "What are you doing here?"

"What do you mean, John?" Mrs. Cherry replied calmly. "This event is open to the public, isn't it?"

Mr. Helmer folded his arms over his chest. "That's right," he said. "No thanks to you and your meddling."

Mrs. Cherry rolled her eyes. "Don't be ridiculous, John," she said. "I was only trying to help. If you'd tried to open this festival without a license, you could have been shut down."

Mr. Helmer shrugged. "Well, you still didn't have to report me to the police," he grumbled.

Nancy's eyes widened. "It sounds like those two have had some problems in the past," she whispered to her friends. "Maybe Mrs. Cherry is trying to ruin Mr. Helmer's festival so more people will go to her orchard."

"I seem to be missing my crop of River Heights Reds," Mr. Helmer said to Mrs. Cherry. "Do you know anything about that?"

"Are you accusing me of something, John?" Mrs. Cherry rolled her eyes and chuckled. "I don't need to take your apples. I have plenty of my own."

Mrs. Cherry turned and moved off. She was still carrying the carved walking stick Nancy had noticed the day before. With each step she leaned on it heavily. Nancy could see that one of the woman's legs was stiff and weak, causing her to limp.

George noticed too. "Hmm," she said quietly. "That hill we saw is pretty steep. Do you think Mrs. Cherry could climb down there?"

"I don't know." Nancy bit her lip thoughtfully. "Maybe not. At least not very easily."

"Maybe she didn't take the apples herself," Bess suggested. "She might have asked someone else to help her."

"Maybe." Nancy shrugged uncertainly. Mrs. Cherry seemed like a nice enough person — not exactly the apple-stealing sort. Then again, Nancy remembered the woman's angry scowl during the applesauce-eating contest the day before. Could she be angry enough at Mr. Helmer to try to ruin his big day?

Just then she noticed that Mr. Helmer was watching them. He was looking at Bess through slightly narrowed eyes, as if trying to remember who she was. Nancy gulped, remembering Bess's comments at the contest.

Bess said she'd do anything for a bushel of those River Heights Reds, Nancy thought worriedly. *Of course, I know she didn't take those apples. But Mr. Helmer doesn't know that. What if he decides that comment makes her a suspect?*

Nancy decided she'd better solve the mystery before that happened. "Come on," she murmured to her friends. "I think it's time to do some investigating."

They hurried off and found a quiet spot behind a nearby food booth. Then Nancy pulled her notebook out of her pocket.

"Okay," she said, flipping it open. "First things first."

She turned to a clean page. At the top, she wrote THE CASE OF THE APPLE BANDIT. Below that, she wrote CLUES.

Bess looked at the page over Nancy's shoulder. "What clues?" she asked.

Nancy chewed on the end of her purple pen. "Well, the apples are missing," she said. "That's a clue, right?"

She wrote:

1. Apples are missing from hiding place.

2. Farm dogs scare away the animals, so the apples were probably stolen by a person.

"That's all I can think of for now," she said. "We'll have to go look for more clues in a minute. First I want to list our suspects." Under SUSPECTS Nancy wrote "Mrs. Cherry" and "wild animals."

George looked doubtful. "I thought we already decided neither one of those suspects could have done it."

"I know," Nancy said. "But until we investigate, we should—"

Her words were interrupted by a loud, sudden shout from nearby.

"You there!" Mr. Helmer yelled. "What are you doing here?"

6
Climbing for Clues

Nancy peered out from behind the food booth. She saw Mr. Helmer standing in front of the two teenage boys who were causing trouble the day before.

"Uh-oh," she told her friends. "I think we might have just found another suspect. Make that *two* suspects."

She couldn't hear what the teens were saying to Mr. Helmer. But she heard Mr. Helmer's voice easily.

"I told you yesterday," he said loudly and sternly, "you're not welcome here. The gate person will refund your money on your way out. And this time, don't come back!"

Nancy watched as the two boys slunk back toward the entrance. Mr. Helmer stayed right behind them, making sure they left.

"Wow," Nancy said. "I wonder what would have happened if Mr. Helmer wasn't right there when those guys came in."

Bess shrugged. "If it gets as crowded as it was yesterday, probably nothing," she guessed. "Those boys could have stayed out of his sight all day, I bet."

"Probably," George agreed. "I wonder why they came back, anyway."

"Hmm," Nancy said.

Bess looked at her with a smile. "I know that look," she teased. "Are you thinking about the mystery?"

"You caught me." Nancy smiled back. Then her face got serious again. "But what if those boys are behind the disappearing apples?"

George gasped. "Oh! Maybe they sneaked in last night and stole the apples to get back at Mr. H for kicking them out!"

"But what about the dogs?" Bess said. "They were guarding the apples last night."

"True," Nancy said. "But those boys were playing with the dogs yesterday, remember? So the dogs probably wouldn't stop them if they sneaked in. They would recognize the boys as friends and let them do whatever they wanted."

She opened her notebook and added the teenage boys to the suspect list. Then she looked over the page. So far they didn't have much to go on.

She snapped her notebook shut and glanced at her friends. "Come on, I think we'd better go check out the scene of the crime."

"You mean climb up that steep hill?" George wrinkled her nose.

Nancy grinned. "Nope," she said. "Let's do it the easy way—climb *down* that steep hill. We can start up by the pony pen."

"All right," Bess agreed. "But let me get a snack first, okay? All this investigating makes me hungry."

"Okay," Nancy said. "But hurry up. The sooner we investigate, the more likely we are to find some clues!"

Nancy and George waited while Bess

bought a shiny red apple and a cup of warm cider at the nearest food booth.

"I just wish this was a River Heights Red," Bess said as she tucked the apple into her jacket pocket. Then she sipped her cider as the girls headed for the hill.

The whole way up to the ponies, Nancy thought about the case. One of the most important parts of any mystery was figuring out the motive—the reason why someone would do something wrong.

"Who has the best motive in this case?" she wondered out loud. "Mrs. Cherry, because she wants her orchard to be the only one? Or those boys, to get back at Mr. Helmer for asking them to leave?"

"How about the raccoons?" George said with a grin. "They have the best motive of all—hunger!"

Just then the girls reached the flat area where the ponies were penned. Bess, who was in the lead, tripped over a rock.

"Oof!" she cried, lurching forward. She caught her balance just in time to keep from falling. But her cider sloshed out of the cup and all over her hand.

"Yuck," George said. "Now you're going to be all sticky."

"It's a good thing your cider was cool," Nancy added.

Bess wrinkled her nose. She hated being dirty or sticky. "Aha," she said, pointing toward the ponies' water tub with her clean hand. "I know where I can wash off."

Nancy giggled. "Good idea," she said. "The ponies will love it—apple-flavored water!"

All three girls walked toward the tub. There were lots of people already lined up for pony rides. H_2O and the other ponies were carrying their riders patiently around the ring. Nancy waved at Marcie, the teenage girl who had been so nice to them yesterday. Marcie waved back and Nancy wished they had time for a ride. But that would have to wait.

"Hurry up and rinse off, Bess," she said, glancing down at the cool, clear water of the tub. "We have work to do!"

Bess reached through the fence and washed off her hand. Then the three friends hurried around the pen to the edge of the drop-off.

"Wow," George said, looking over the edge. "This looks really steep."

"We'll have to go slowly and be careful," Nancy said. "I'll go first. . . ."

The girls made their way down the hill. It was a slow trip—they had to slip-slide down the steep path, holding on to branches and saplings to keep their balance. There were roots everywhere trying to trip them up, and lots of slippery patches of mud and slick, wet leaves.

"Yikes," Bess panted. "Who would go to all this trouble just to climb down here and snatch some apples?"

"Or up," George added. "They might have climbed up."

Nancy shook her head as she wriggled between a couple of bushes. "Either way, it's not an easy trip," she said. "I mean, Mr. Helmer probably just sent a few of his young workers down here with the apples. But it would take a lot of effort for someone to come down and drag them away."

"Not for a raccoon," George pointed out. "Maybe it's too hard for Mr. Helmer's dogs to get down here too. That would mean the wild animals could be the culprits after all."

Nancy was about to agree when she heard a bark. Glancing down, she saw two of Mr. Helmer's dogs leaping up the slope toward them. They moved across the difficult ground as easily as if they were romping in the grassy yard.

"Wrong," Bess told her cousin. "Looks like the dogs don't have any trouble getting here."

Nancy finally reached the flat area where they had seen the apple baskets. She stretched her arms, relieved. Then she reached down to pat one of the dogs, who was sniffing curiously at her feet.

"No, I don't think we can blame wild animals," she said. "Not only because of the dogs. But wild animals wouldn't eat the apple baskets."

"Oh, yeah." George flopped onto the ground beside her. "Yuck!" she cried, springing up almost immediately.

"Ew, your pants are all muddy!" Bess said, helping her brush off.

Nancy didn't pay any attention. She was staring at the second dog. He had just picked up a large fallen branch. As she watched, he leaped up the hillside carrying it in his mouth.

"Hey," she said. "I have another theory. Bess, do you still have that apple?"

Bess put a hand over her pocket. "Yes," she said. "Why?"

"Can I have it, please? It's important," Nancy begged.

Bess looked reluctant. But she pulled out the apple and handed it over.

Nancy bent down in front of the first dog. "Here, boy," she said. "Want this? Yum yum!"

"Hey!" Bess protested.

But Nancy ignored her. "Yummy apple!" she cooed, pressing the fruit to the dog's muzzle.

The dog sniffed at it. But he didn't even try to lick or bite it. Meanwhile the second dog returned. Nancy tried to feed the apple to him, too. But he wasn't interested either.

"Oh, well," she said at last. She stood up and handed the apple back to Bess.

Bess snatched it and shoved it back into her pocket. "Whew!" she said. "What did you do that for?"

"I thought maybe the farm dogs took the apples," Nancy explained. "They could have eaten them, and then carried off the baskets somewhere." She shrugged. "Sort of the way Chip likes to carry off Dad's socks and my pencils and bury them in the yard."

George nodded. "Good thinking," she said. "But I bet Mr. Helmer trained his dogs not to eat apples. Or else they just don't like the taste."

Bess glanced up the hill. "I know who likes the taste of apples," she said. "Ponies."

"Yeah," Nancy said. "But there's no way the ponies could climb down here. Not even if they could break out of their pen."

She sighed. So far this mystery wasn't very easy to solve. She and her friends spent a few more minutes looking around for clues. But there weren't any. No footprints, no nothing.

"So I guess our only suspects are still Mrs. Cherry and those boys," George commented as the girls started the climb back up toward the pony pen. "Even if we can't prove either one did it."

Nancy bit her lip instead of answering. She had just thought of one other suspect: Chip.

7

A Hopeless Case?

Nancy thought about her new idea as she climbed back up the steep hill. Could Chip possibly be the apple bandit?

George's mom said she chased Chip around for half an hour, she thought uncertainly. *Is that enough time? Could Chip eat or hide that many apples in half an hour? And still have time to drag away the baskets?*

She didn't think so. But she couldn't be sure. Chip loved to hide the rolled-up socks when Hannah did the laundry.

Nancy decided not to say anything to her friends yet. If they didn't find the real apple bandit soon, she would mention it.

"Now what?" George asked as she reached the top of the hill, panting.

"Snack time?" Bess asked hopefully. "I really want to try that apple soup I saw at the food stand. . . ."

"Not yet," Nancy said. "First I want to talk to the pony workers. Whoever took those apples would either have to cross the stream and climb up, or climb down from here. Maybe they saw something suspicious last night or this morning."

"Good point." George nodded.

They walked over to the pony pen. Marcie was taking a break, leaning on the fence near the hay pile while the other teenage girls led the ponies.

"Hi," Marcie said when Nancy and her friends came over. "Did you guys come back for another ride?"

"Not exactly." Nancy took a deep breath. "Did you hear about the missing apples?"

"The what?" The older girl looked confused.

Nancy and her friends quickly explained about the hiding place down the hill. Then they told her what Mr. Helmer had said

57

earlier, and about their own search for clues.

"Wow!" Marcie said when they were finished. She glanced toward the drop-off. "I didn't even know there was anything hidden down there in the first place."

"So you didn't see anyone climbing down there last night?" Nancy asked. "Or early this morning, maybe?"

Marcie shrugged. "The only ones I've seen climb down there are you guys." She laughed. "I thought you were nuts when I saw you doing that earlier! I didn't realize you were trying to solve a mystery."

Nancy nodded. "Um, are you sure you didn't see anyone else?"

"Nobody." Marcie shook her head. "We left last night pretty soon after you guys did. We got here early this morning to feed and water the ponies and clean up the pen. But there was nobody around then."

"Okay." Nancy sighed, disappointed. "Thanks anyway."

"Good luck with your mystery." The older girl waved and headed back to work.

Nancy and her friends walked back

down the hill to the main part of the festival. "This is a tough one," Nancy admitted. "We don't really have any clues at all. There are no good suspects, and nobody saw anything suspicious. . . ."

"It's like those apples just disappeared into thin air," Bess said.

"Or into a raccoon's stomach," George added. "I still think that's probably what happened. The raccoons might have dragged away the baskets, too."

"Maybe," Nancy said. But she didn't really believe George's theory. She had a hunch that something else was behind the missing apples. But what?

"So what do we do now?" George asked. "We already looked for clues and wrote down all the suspects. What more can we do?"

"Maybe we should just think about it for a while," Bess suggested hopefully. "You know—while we get some snacks and walk around the festival and stuff."

"I guess we might as well try to have fun." Nancy bit her lower lip. "I can't think of anything else to do to solve this case. Well, except to watch out for anything suspicious."

"We can do that," Bess said. "Now come on, let's go have fun!"

For the next two hours, Nancy did her best to enjoy herself. She joined her friends in tasting some delicious apple fritters and cider. Then they all went on a hayride, explored a maze made out of hay bales, picked themselves a bushel of fresh apples right off the trees in the orchard, and even went dunking for apples in a barrel of cider. There were lots of people at the festival enjoying the sunny fall day, and the girls ran into several people they knew from school.

The three friends were just finishing up a tasty lunch of hot dogs and apple juice when they heard a loud cheer erupt from over by the farmhouse.

"What's going on over there?" Bess wondered.

"Oh!" George glanced at her watch. "It must be the finals for the applesauce-eating contest. They're supposed to be starting right now. I saw it on the information board this morning."

"Let's go watch," Bess said. "I want to see if that skinny kid who won my heat wins the whole thing."

The girls hurried over and found spots with a good view of the front of the farmhouse. The long table was still set up on the porch. This time about a dozen people of all ages were seated behind it, from young kids to adults. The skinny kid from Bess's heat was right in the middle.

"All right, bring out the applesauce!" Mr. Helmer was saying into the microphone. "Let the games begin!"

Orchard workers appeared with their loaded trays. But Nancy was barely paying attention as the contest began, even though Bess and George were shouting and cheering beside her. She was too busy thinking about the mystery.

It just seems impossible to solve, she thought. *Could Mrs. Cherry really be mad enough at Mr. Helmer to want to ruin his festival? It seems kind of crazy. Plus I don't think she could climb up or down that steep hill with her bad leg.*

Next she thought about the teenage boys.

They had seemed pretty angry about being kicked out of the festival.

But would they really sneak in here last night and do something so mean? she wondered. *I guess it's possible. Maybe they fed all the apples to the ponies and then threw away the baskets. But how did they know where the apples were hidden in the first place?*

She sighed, staring at the contestants on the porch. They were all still busy shoveling applesauce into their mouths.

I wish Marcie and the other pony workers had stayed overnight with the ponies, she thought. *Maybe then they would have seen or heard something. Especially since whoever did it probably climbed down rather than up—that would be a lot easier since the hill was so muddy and slippery. Of course, it would still be awfully hard to climb down there in the dark. . . .*

She noticed a teenage boy standing nearby, cheering loudly for one of the applesauce eaters. But when she looked more closely at him, she realized it wasn't one of the suspects. That made sense, since Mr. Helmer had kicked them out.

Maybe we should try to find them, though, Nancy thought. *If we could figure out where they live, we could go and check them out. If they're the culprits, their shoes might still be muddy, unless they stopped to rinse them off in the ponies' tub or something. . . .*

She was distracted by a sudden extra-loud cheer. Then Mr. Helmer's voice came over the microphone.

"We have a winner!" he cried. He walked over to the skinny red-haired boy. "Congratulations, young man!"

"Wow!" Bess exclaimed. "Now I don't feel so bad—he even beat the grown-ups!"

Mr. Helmer had the boy stand up and take a bow. "Thank you, thank you!" the kid said happily. "So do I get my prize now? I'm hungry!"

The audience laughed. But Mr. Helmer looked upset.

"I'm sorry, son," he said. "I know I promised you a bushel of River Heights Reds. Unfortunately the apples seem to have disappeared sometime last night, so I'm afraid I won't be able to—"

"Hold on!" Nancy cried, loudly enough for everyone to hear. The answer had just clicked into her mind. It was so clear all of a sudden. "I think I know what happened to those apples!"

8

An Unexpected Answer

Bess and George turned to stare at her. "Huh?" George said.

"What are you talking about?" Bess added.

Mr. Helmer was peering at her from the porch. "What was that, young lady?" he asked. "Do you really know something about my missing apples?"

"I—I think so." Nancy suddenly felt a little shy. Everyone in the crowd and up on the porch was staring at her. But she stood up straight and tall. "Please, just come with me. I'll show you what I think happened."

She could tell that the orchard owner was confused. Her friends looked stumped too. But Nancy knew it would be better to show them than to tell them. Besides, she needed to check one thing before she knew her solution was right.

Nancy led them all up the hill to the pony pen. The teenage girls were still marching the ponies around in circles, though they all stopped when they saw the crowd approaching.

"What's going on?" Marcie asked, leading her pony to the fence.

Nancy walked up to her. "Hi," she said. "Remember that mystery we were telling you about? Um, I think I just solved it."

"Cool!" Marcie said. "So who dunnit?"

"First I need to ask you a very important question," Nancy told her.

The older girl looked alarmed. "Hey, wait a minute," she said. "You don't think I stole the apples, do you? I told you, I didn't even know they were down there."

"I know." Nancy smiled to reassure her. "That's sort of what the question is about. Can you tell me exactly what you guys did to take care of the ponies last night and this morning?" She waved her hand to include the other pony workers.

Marcie shrugged. "Sure," she said. "You saw what we were doing last night. We just put out some more hay and took off the ponies' saddles. Then we left."

"And this morning?" Nancy urged.

Mr. Helmer stepped forward. "Is this going somewhere?" he asked, sounding a little impatient.

Nancy nodded. "Please," she said. "This is the important part of the question."

Marcie shrugged again. "Like I told you before, we got here early," she said. "We brought a little more hay up from the truck in a wheelbarrow. Then those two cleaned out the pen and used the empty wheelbarrow to take away the, um, pony poo."

"Is that all?" Nancy prompted. "What about the water tub?"

"Oh!" the older girl said. "That's right. We also dumped out the water—H-Two-Oh had dunked his hay in it last night, so it was all mucky. We filled it again from one of the irrigation hoses." She glanced at

68

Mr. Helmer. "You told us we could do that."

Mr. Helmer nodded. Nancy smiled. Now she knew she'd solved the case. "Okay, but *where* did you dump out the old water?" she asked.

"We tipped it over the edge of the—oh!" Marcie exclaimed. Her hand flew to her face. "We dumped it right down the hillside," she said. "Right about where you guys climbed down earlier."

Mr. Helmer gasped. "Oh!" he cried, looking over at the large water tub. "It must have washed away my apples!" He called to a couple of young orchard workers. "Run down to the creek and see if the baskets floated downstream," he told them.

As the workers ran off, George stared at Nancy. "How in the world did you figure that one out?" she exclaimed.

"Yes," Mr. Helmer said curiously. "I'd like to know that too."

Nancy smiled. "I was thinking about it some more during the applesauce contest," she explained. "That was when I finally put together some weird facts. Like how it hasn't rained in weeks, but there was mud and wet plants and stuff all the way down the hillside. Remember?"

"Yeah." Bess looked down at her sneakers. They were still muddy from the climb. "I didn't even think about that."

"I also remembered that the water in the ponies' tub was clean this morning," Nancy said. "You even rinsed your hand off in it, Bess."

"But last night it was already all gunky from H-Two-Oh's hay," George said, nodding thoughtfully.

"H-Two-Oh?" Mr. Helmer said, looking confused.

The girls explained about the hay-dunking pony. "They're right," Marcie put in. "We have to dump and refill the tub every day because of H-Two-Oh's messy habit."

"So anyway, I finally put two and two together," Nancy said. "Especially since there didn't seem to be a way that anyone else could have done it. I realized what must have really happened."

They talked about it a little more while they waited for the orchard workers to return. When they did, the workers were riding in a little cart that held several soggy wooden baskets—and a lot of wet, slimy-looking apples!

"We found them, boss!" one of the workers cried. "They were stuck in the rocks about a hundred yards downstream."

"Yay!" George cheered. "Nancy solved the mystery!"

"Don't sound so happy," Bess said. "Most of the apples are ruined."

Mr. Helmer smiled and patted her on the head. "That's okay," he said. "I can grow more apples. I'm just happy to know there's not a thief skulking around my orchard."

"I'm really sorry about this," Marcie spoke up. "It's all our fault."

"Nonsense." Mr. Helmer shook his head. "You had no way of knowing the apples were down there. I just hid them too well!" He laughed loudly at his own joke. Then, to prove there were no hard feelings, he offered the wet and bruised apples to the ponies.

"Thanks!" Marcie said. "They don't care what they look like. Right, H-Two-Oh?"

The little spotted pony had come over to the fence to see what was happening. When Nancy offered him an apple, he crunched it eagerly in his teeth.

Bess laughed. "Look, he loves the River Heights Red too!"

"Obviously a pony of taste," Mr. Helmer said with a smile. Then he turned his smile toward Nancy. "I want to thank you, young lady. As soon as I harvest some more River Heights Reds, I want to give you a bushel as a way of saying thank you."

"Hey!" Bess exclaimed. "I helped too!"

Everyone laughed, especially Nancy. "Don't worry, Bess," she said. "We'll split the apples. After all, we're a team!"

By bedtime that night, Nancy was so tired her eyes were almost falling shut. It had been a long, fun day at the Apple Festival. But before she went to bed, she pulled out her detective notebook to finish writing up the case.

The Case of the Apple Bandit was a juicy mystery—and a tricky one, too.

There were hardly any good suspects, and at first it seemed like there were no clues at all.

But the clues were there—we just didn't recognize them at first. It just goes to show that even something that seems normal at first can be a clue. Like a muddy hillside on a dry day. Or a tub full of clear water near a messy pony.

Anyway, I'm glad I figured it out in the end. It made a fun day at the Apple Festival even better—especially since Bess, George, and I all got free pony rides afterward, along with being promised a free bushel of apples. Now that's what I call a tasty reward!

Case closed!